LEGACY PRESS®

An imprint of Rose Publishing, Inc.
Torrance, CA
www.Rose-Publishing.com

Read more about your favorite tusked detective
in these Bill the Warthog Mysteries:

Book 1
Full Metal Trench Coat

Book 2
Guarding the Tablets of Stone

Book 3
Attack of the Mutant Fruit

Book 4
Quest for the Temple of Truth

Book 5
The Bogus Mind Machine

Book 6
King Con

Book 7
The Case of the Campfire Caper

Bill the Warthog MYSTERIES

ATTACK of the MUTANT FRUIT

Dean A. Anderson

*Thanks to Christy and Kristen for their editing
expertise – and to DaddyRob for his fishing advice.*

BILL THE WARTHOG MYSTERIES: ATTACK OF THE MUTANT FRUIT
©2013 by Dean Anderson, eighth printing
ISBN 10: 1-58411-078-3
ISBN 13: 978-1-58411-078-1
Legacy reorder# LP48303
JUVENILE FICTION / Religion / Children

LegacyPress
An imprint of Rose Publishing, Inc.
4733 Torrance Blvd., #259
Torrance, CA 90503
www.Rose-Publishing.com

Cover and Interior Illustrator: Dave Carleson

Scriptures are from the *Holy Bible: New International Version*
(North American Edition), ©1973, 1978, 1984 by the International
Bible Society. Used by permission of Zondervan Bible Publishers.

Printed in the United States of America

Table of Contents

Chapter 1

The Case of the Maltese Fruit

Brandon Hoover chewed a mean stick of gum. But what he did even better was blow bubbles.

He didn't just blow big bubbles; he blew unusual bubbles. Sure, he could blow a bubble as big as his face, but the other tricks he could do were astounding.

Brandon could blow a bubble in a bubble in a bubble. He could blow a bubble in the shape of a banana or, on occasion, in the shape of a cube.

You would think a talent like that would make Brandon the most unusual kid in town, but he wasn't. That would probably be me. There are a couple of different things about me.

For one, I was the best kid around at playing video

games, so my friends started insisting I play video games with my feet. Now they call me "Ten Toes," Nick "Ten Toes" Sayga (and I still beat them at video games, but the scores are a little closer).

But the really unusual thing about me is my best friend. He's kind of my boss, too. He's a warthog.

Now don't think I'm being mean, calling a friend a name. He really is a warthog, and his name is Bill. Bill tries to fit in by wearing clothes and walking on his hind feet. He is more comfortable on all fours, though.

Bill is a detective. If you know books, it might help to think of Bill as Sherlock Holmes and me as Watson.

We solve cases, and Brandon Hoover brought us a case, even though he didn't know it. He came to my house when Bill was over chewing the fat. ("Chewing the fat" was an expression Bill used for talking. Actually, he was chewing on some weeds in my backyard.)

"Hey Nick," Brandon called.

"I'm back here," I shouted, and Brandon came through our back gate.

"Nick, I . . . Whoa!" You should have seen the look on Brandon's face when he saw Bill. I thought he was going to swallow his gum.

8

"Brandon, this is my friend Bill. I'm sure you've heard about him, so don't freak."

"Yeah, I heard about him, but, as I said, 'Whoa!'"

It was a warm day, so Bill wasn't wearing his trench coat, just slacks and a short-sleeved white button-down shirt. He offered Brandon a hoof.

"Good to meet you, Brandon, I'm Bill."

"Um, good to meet you," Brandon stammered. He looked back at me. "Hey Nick, I have something amazing to tell you. Can I talk about it around your, um, friend?"

"Anything you have to tell me, you can tell Bill," I said.

"OK, Nick," Brandon said. "Well, I go through a lot of gum, at least a couple of packs a day."

"Sugarless, I hope?" Bill inquired.

"At least four out of five packs are, dentist's orders," Brandon assured him. "Anyway, I have a great new source. Chris Franklin's got a plant that grows gum. You've got to see it."

Bill looked at me, and I knew we would have to see it. Bill and I had dealt with Chris many times before, and with him there was always an angle – usually a crooked one.

So Brandon, Bill and I headed for Chris's house. He didn't seem happy to see Bill and me, but he tried to cover it with a fake smile. "I see Brandon has told you about our little discovery, our *secret* discovery."

"Aw, come on now, Chris," Brandon said. "An investment opportunity like this is too good to keep to ourselves. Nick's a good guy, and I thought he should be able to get in on it."

"Investment opportunity?" Bill's ears were pointing straight up.

"I guess it wouldn't hurt to let a few more people in on this. And I do mean people," Chris said, looking right at Bill. "I'll show you the greenhouse."

We went to Chris's backyard and there was a little greenhouse. It was one of those places made of tinted glass for growing plants.

Inside the small space it was warmer even than outside. There were a lot of plants, but we couldn't help noticing one little plant on a high shelf with some signs posted near it. One sign said "Do not touch!" and the other signs said, "Stay away! Plant sensitive!" The plant seemed to be sprouting large gumballs.

"I see you've noticed our little secret," Chris said to me. "This is a rare plant from the island of Malta. It was cultivated there years ago by scientists for the King of Malta.

"The King loved gum, so they developed this plant that grew a fruit that is in every way like gum balls. This plant has been kept in the Maltese royal line as a secret, but my uncle, an ambassador to Malta, managed to smuggle one out of the country.

"These are delicate plants, and before you ask, I'm telling you, Mr. Detective, that you cannot examine it up close. You'd probably eat it, and you don't have the expertise to examine it anyway.

"I've been studying horticulture (that's the science of growing plants to you, Warthog) and believe that we can, with a little financial assistance, mass produce these plants and make a fortune."

"Brandon, how much are you investing in this so-called opportunity?" Bill asked.

"Fifty dollars, for now," Brandon said. "But I'm hoping to get my parents to cash some college savings bonds so I can invest more."

"Before you invest more, perhaps we better be sure that Chris has the expertise in horticulture to

handle this project," Bill said.

"Oh, I have the expertise," Chris said. "This greenhouse is my mom's, but I've spent hour after hour out here cultivating vegetables like carrots, tomatoes, avocados, spinach, kiwis and Brussels sprouts, and fruit like strawberries and watermelon. I know what I'm doing."

"I know what you're doing, too," said Bill. "It's called fraud, and you really ought to spend less time with this kind of deceit and instead learn about the fruit of the Spirit."

How was Bill sure Chris was lying (besides the fact his lips were moving) and what is this fruit of the Spirit?

☞ **Turn to page 88 to find out!**

Chapter 2

The Case of the Counterfeit Valentines

Jacob showed me the valentine. It wasn't a pleasant sight.

> Ashley – You are so cute! I like you a lot and was wondering if maybe we could go out some time. Call me. Your teddy bear, Jacob.

"Why are you showing this to me, Jacob? I just ate."

"You don't understand, Nick," Jacob said. "I didn't write it, it came with this other note. Both were stuck in my lunch bag." He showed me the second note.

> Jacob – If you don't put five dollars in the knothole of the big playground oak tree at 3:00 PM the day before Valentine's Day, Ashley Bartlett will receive this note.

"Nasty stuff," I said. "Unless you do like Ashley, in which case . . ."

"Don't even joke about this, Nick. Besides, I'm not the only one. Tito, Colin, Bobby, a bunch of guys got similar notes threatening to send valentines to different girls."

"I wonder why I didn't get one."

"Maybe whoever did this is afraid to blackmail someone with a detective friend."

"Is there anyone you suspect?"

"Well, Ryan Hodgkins was seen by the lunch bag cabinet. And he's probably trying to raise money."

"You're right! The NWL is coming to town."

The NWL is the National Wrestling League, and Ryan is a huge fan of the NWL star Digger Graves. Ryan was sure to be trying to get money for tickets and souvenirs.

Jacob and I headed for Bill's office and knocked on his door.

"Come in," came from behind the door. Bill was leaning back on his swivel chair, his hind feet propped up on his desk.

"Hey, Nick," Bill said. "Just reading a letter from the Thompsons."

16

"Isn't that the family that rescued you from the Pottersville Zoo and raised you?" I asked.

"Of course. Sometimes I think how different life would have been without the Thompson family. I wouldn't have read mystery stories, sung hymns, or learned to floss.

"Say, who's your friend?"

"Bill, this is Jacob. We need to introduce you to someone named Ryan."

Jacob told his story on the walk to the Hodgkins' house.

"I don't see why you can't just tell her the note isn't from you," Bill said.

Jacob and I shook our heads in disgust.

"You just can't do that, Bill," I said, "What would he say to Ashley? 'The note says I like you, but really I hate your guts'?"

"Yeah, Bill," Jacob said. "It's hard to tell someone you don't 'like' them, especially if you like them. I don't care about me looking stupid, but I don't want Ashley's feelings to be hurt."

"There is none of this confusion in the warthog world, I'll tell you," said Bill.

Fortunately, we were at Ryan's house by this time.

I knocked on the door. Ryan invited us in, and we went back to his bedroom. There were Digger Graves posters all over the walls.

"So, I hear you're a big fan of this wrestling fellow," Bill ventured.

"Digger Graves is the coolest guy on earth. I am so looking forward to his coming to town," Ryan said.

"I hear the tickets for the event are expensive," Bill said.

"Yeah," said Ryan. "But I'll get the money to go. I think my grandma will give me money. Yeah, that's it. My grandma."

I saw Jacob staring at Ryan's desk. On top of it was a big pile of envelopes. Jacob whispered in Bill's ear.

"So what are those letters on your desk, Ryan? Jacob tells me the envelopes look familiar."

"Oh, those," shrugged Ryan. "I'm president of the local Digger Graves fan club, and I wanted to send letters to all the members to make sure they come to the NWL event to support the Diggster."

"Could I look at one of those letters?" Bill asked.

"Oh, um, no," Ryan said. "They're sealed already."

"But you haven't got around to addressing and stamping them yet."

"Oh, I'll get to that. I'm waiting till next week to get the stamps."

"Why next week?" I asked.

"Don't you know anything?" Ryan exclaimed. "The United States Post Office is putting out a Digger Graves stamp next week! So I've been waiting to stamp the letters till those come out."

"Really," said Bill. "These will be official United States government stamps?"

"You bet," Ryan said. "They're going to honor three other wrestling heroes, too. Mad Dog Lewbowski, The Boulder, and Mortimer 'Polite' Henderson will all get stamps. Congress is going to have a big ceremony next week to honor them when the stamps come out."

"Hmmm," Bill muttered. "Stamps are interesting things. I've thought of joining a Philatelic Society."

"What?" I asked.

"Stamp collecting club. Did you know you can still use any valid United States postal stamp that has been printed since 1861, at its labeled value? By the way, Ryan, you've canceled out any hope of our believing your story.

"I believe there is something very different in those envelopes, Ryan. I believe that in those envelopes are the phony love letters you are using to blackmail other students at Elm Street Elementary."

"How dare you say that!" exclaimed Ryan. "I've told nothing but the truth."

"Obviously not. But you have given the evidence to stamp out your little plot."

Bill whispered something to Ryan, and he handed all of the envelopes over to Bill. They were indeed the fake valentines. After Jacob went home, Bill told me how he knew for sure Ryan was lying. Then he said something that surprised me.

"I know those love letters were phony, but I think Jacob was showing love for Ashley by keeping the letter from her. Not the mushy kind of love, but the fruit of the Spirit kind of love."

What was Bill's proof that Ryan was lying? And what kind of love was Bill talking about?

☞ Turn to page 90 to find out!

Chapter 3

The Case of the Stolen Jokes

Steven Martinski always had a joke on hand, perhaps because he always had a joke book on hand. *Light Bulb Repair Made Difficult, 101 Llama Jokes, The Truth behind the Chickens and the Roadways,* or another one of many joke books was always in his hand or his back pocket.

I knew Steven was greatly looking forward to the school talent show, so I was surprised when he knocked on my door the day of the talent show auditions.

"Nick," he said, obviously out of breath, "I just flew in from school, and boy, are my arms tired."

"Come on in, Steven."

"You'll need to contact your detective friend. There's been a theft."

"What was stolen, Steven? Your bike? Joke books? Not your video game system?" (I myself often have nightmares about my Gamemastersquare 3000 being taken away.)

"No, nothing like that. Jared Prentiss stole my act!"

I invited Steven in, got him a glass of water and had him sit down. He had run all the way from school. I called Bill and when Bill got to the house, Steven told us his story.

"Thanks for coming, Mr. Warthog. I'll need to start my story a month ago, when the talent show auditions were announced."

Steven told us he had been working since then, going through his joke books and adapting the jokes to our school. He turned a selection of airline food jokes into Elm Street Elementary School cafeteria jokes. He also worked on some good-natured jokes about the teachers and office staff.

He wrote all the jokes in a notebook. But last week, he said, his notebook turned up missing from his desk for a day. The next day, the notebook was back. Steven had wondered what happened to it.

"Now I know what happened," Steven said. "Jared Prentiss must have taken my notebook and copied my act. I know because he was doing my exact act at the audition."

"Well, Steven," I said, "couldn't it be coincidence? After all, you don't do original jokes, you get them from joke books."

"But I adapted the jokes for the show. For instance, Jared took this joke word for word from my notebook: 'What's black and white and red all over? Principal Kingstone's Dalmatian with chicken pox.'"

"That does sound more than suspicious," Bill said. "Let's go down to the school and check this out."

When we got to school, the auditions were still taking place in the gym. Mrs. Newberry, the school secretary, met us at the door.

"Oh, Steven," said Mrs. Newberry, "you were scheduled to audition earlier, but we can still fit you in. And Nick," she added, looking at me and then at Bill, "I'm afraid we aren't allowing animal acts this year. But what a cute job you did dressing up your dog. And teaching him to walk on his hind legs, that's just adorable!"

I could tell that Bill wanted to let Mrs. Newberry's

comment pass, and Steven spotted Jared, so we went to talk to him.

"Steven!" greeted Jared, "Did you catch my act?"

"You mean my act," said Steven.

"Hey, Nick," said Jared. "So this is the warthog pig everyone's talking about."

"Actually, the pig is a different species," said Bill.

"No," said Jared, "I meant it like how some people call police 'pigs,' so like you're a detective. Maybe I could call you a 'Pig Pig.' I need to work that into my act."

"Police officers consider it highly offensive to be called 'pig,'" said Bill. "I don't exactly see why, but since they don't like it, it should not be used."

"I don't know," said Steven. "It would be the only original joke in your act."

"What do you mean by that?" Jared said. "My act is my own. I wouldn't be surprised to see you steal my jokes, though. I'll have to watch your audition to make sure you don't."

"Like you came up with that 'black and white and red all over' joke," said Steven. "I've been studying that genre of joke for years."

(Bill whispered to me that 'genre' was a category

or type of stuff.)

"Oh yeah?" said Jared. "Well, I've been working on that kind of joke for years myself."

I had an idea. "Hey, Steven, Jared, since you claim  to be experts, why don't we have a contest to see who runs out of answers to 'what's black and white and red all over' jokes first?"

They agreed, so I asked, "What's black and white and red all over?"

"A sunburned penguin," Steven said.

Jared thought a moment, then said, "A zebra with diaper rash."

"An embarrassed Oreo," Steven shot back.

"Ah, um, a panda with a bloody nose," Jared responded.

"Snoopy, after an accident painting his dog house," said Steven, which made Jared laugh.

"A police car after it crashed into the tomato truck," Jared said, which got a chuckle out of Steven.

"I think you two could go on for a very long time," said Bill. "But since you both say you know all about these kinds of jokes, let's see who knows the original

29

answer to the riddle."

Bill gave both Steven and Jared a slip of paper and a pencil. They both wrote something down. Bill looked at the papers.

"Well," said Bill, "Steven has the correct answer, and I think the evidence points to the act being his. But there is something more important at stake here."

"What could that be?" Steven asked.

"More important than who gets the credit, is the Holy Spirit's fruit of joy. Toward the end of your contest you were beginning to enjoy each other. Perhaps you two could do an act together for the talent show."

Steven and Jared took Bill's advice, and they won the talent show contest. With part of the prize money, they got Bill fake glasses with a big nose and mustache. (I'm afraid the disguise wouldn't fool any bad guys, but it was funny.)

What was the answer that Steven wrote on the paper? And what is the fruit of joy?

☞ Turn to page 92 to find out!

Chapter 4

Phil the Warthog Goes West

Whenever Mike Reed drew a new *Phil the Warthog* comic, he always showed it to Bill first. He wouldn't admit it, but Phil was obviously based on Bill, so Mike always went to Bill for comments.

The character Phil the Warthog was a genetically engineered project made by a mad scientist: a talking warthog. A government agent had rescued Phil. Phil also had a time machine.

(Bill always complained, "Why can't he draw comics of ordinary warthogs pursuing ordinary tasks? Caring for their young, searching for grass, decorating the new aardvark burrow . . .")

The new issue did have an interesting setting: *Phil*

the Warthog in the Wild West. Apparently, in a previous issue, as Phil the Warthog was trying to travel back in time to find the origin of the common cold, he accidentally stranded himself in the American West of the 1870s. Phil had taken the job of sheriff in the small Western town of Nowheresville.

The first panel showed Phil wearing western gear, from the ten-gallon hat on his head to the cowboy boots on his bottom hooves. He was tilting back in a chair in the sheriff's office, boots on the desk.

In the next panel, a man in overalls burst through the door.

PHIL: Now slow down, pardner. What in tarnation is your hurry, Farmer McCoy?

FARMER MCCOY: It's them Blackhate Boys. They tore down my fence and drove their cattle through my land to the old water hole.

PHIL: All right, let's ride out and look at the damage.

Several panels were devoted to Phil's unsuccessful attempt to mount a horse. Eventually he joined Farmer McCoy on his wagon and the two rode out to the McCoy farm.

The next panels showed damaged fruit trees and a wheat field trampled by cattle.

PHIL: Did you see the men driving the cattle?

FARMER McCOY: No, but I did see the brand. And who beside the Blackhate Boys would do such a thing?

The next panel showed Farmer McCoy and Phil riding back into town. Leaning against the front wall of the general store was a man dressed all in black.

FARMER McCOY: Look, Sheriff Phil, it's Bart Blackhate!

Phil climbed out of the wagon and faced Bart Blackhate.

PHIL: Bart, I understand you've been driving your cattle rather carelessly.

BART: What business is my cattle driving to you, you dirty, lowdown, pig farmer?

PHIL: Well, I may be a tad filthy; it's hard to find good bathing facilities in these parts. As to being lowdown, I could understand your saying that if I was walking on all fours, but as you can see I take great care to walk on my hind hooves.

BART: I just meant—

PHIL: I know you meant to be insulting, but I'll still address the issues you raised. Whether you were calling me a farmer who raised pigs or a pig who farms, either would be inaccurate. I am a warthog and a sheriff, while you are a lawbreaker.

BART: You got no right to call me a lawbreaker without proof.

PHIL: Perhaps I did speak hastily. Farmer McCoy, what brand did you see on the cattle that came through your land?

FARMER MCCOY: It was an "X," then another "X," and both were underlined.

BART: Now see there, that proves it wasn't my family's cattle. Our ranch is the Bar Twenty ranch and our brand is the Bar Twenty.

The panel showed Bart's hand getting close to the gun in the holster on his hip.

FARMER MCCOY: Oh, your brand is Bar Twenty? Perhaps there was some misunderstanding.

PHIL: There was no misunderstanding. I'm sure those cows were the Blackhates'. So, Bart, you'll either be paying for the damage your cattle did, or you'll be going to jail.

BART: I won't be doing either.

The next panel showed Bart drawing his gun.

The next panel showed Phil drawing some strange,

science fiction laser gun. The ray from Phil's device focused on Bart's gun, and Bart's gun vanished.

BART: Where did you get the new-fangled piece?

PHIL: From the East. But you should be worrying less about my piece here, and more about the fruit of peace.

BART: I'm worried about getting my cattle watered.

FARMER McCOY: Well, if you had just asked, I could help you make a path through my land that won't disturb my crops.

BART: I reckon we could make a deal. After we pay for the damages.

PHIL: Well, now that we've solved that, I can get back to working on my time problem.

BART AND FARMER McCOY: What was that?

PHIL: I said I can get back to working on the crime problem.

Bill closed the comic.

"So, what did you think?" Mike asked.

"Interesting," Bill said. "I am a little uncomfortable with the mix of science fiction and western genres, particularly that laser gun from the future. But I always am struck by how good looking the character Phil is."

"I didn't get the ending," I said. "How did Phil know that the cattle belonged to the Blackhates?"

"That was elementary," said Bill. "I was pleased that Phil addressed the issue of peace. Much more important than Farmer McCoy's fruit trees, is the issue of the fruit of peace."

How did Phil know the cattle belonged to the Blackhates? And what is the fruit of peace?

☞ Turn to page 94 to find out!

Chapter 5

The Case of the Magnetic Bait

"For the billionth time, Bill, I'm not taking you," I said.

We were in Bill's office. Bill was trying to talk me into bringing him along to the Chuck Jones Reservoir Fishing Contest. The last three times I tried to go fishing with Bill, he ate all the bait before we got to the fishing hole.

"Why not, Nick?" Bill asked.

"You know why," I said.

"It was just a worm or two," Bill said.

"It was more than a worm or two."

"Well, the last time we went to the movies, you ate all the M&Ms during the coming attractions."

I was about to explain that it wasn't the same thing at all when Sawyer Tomson came in the door.

"Do you know anything about magnetism?" Sawyer asked.

"Who are you?" Bill asked.

"Bill, this is Sawyer Tomson. He's in my class. Sawyer, this is Bill the Warthog, Private Investigator."

"Good to meet you," Bill said. "Magnetism?"

"Yeah, Sawyer," I said. "Slow down and tell us the whole story."

It wasn't the first time Sawyer had been told to slow down. He wasn't the most patient person in the world, except when he was fishing.

Sawyer was great at fishing. He knew when and where to go on a lake or stream, and what bait and line to pick. Most of all, he was patient waiting for the fish to bite and patient at reeling them in.

"Dwayne Peacock says he's going to beat me in the fishing contest. He says he's going to win through the power of magnetism."

Dwayne was one of Chris Franklin's posse, so I knew Bill and I would be talking to him soon.

On the way to Dwayne's house, Bill agreed something fishy (sorry) was afoot. According to

Sawyer, Dwayne claimed that he had a miracle magnet that would attract record numbers of fish.

Dwayne was telling other kids that he would sell them magnets like his after he proved the magnet's worth by winning the fishing contest.

We knocked on the door and Dwayne answered.

"Well, Nick . . . and Porky. I suppose you want to see my fish magnet."

"We were interested," Bill said. "For science's sake."

"You just want to steal its secrets so you can win the contest. Well, you can't. You can buy one like any other kid at school after I win the contest."

He slammed the door.

"This could be an interesting case," I said.

"True," Bill said. "I'm afraid I'll have to go to that fishing contest after all."

The Chuck Jones Reservoir was dug about ten years ago. They seeded it with fish, and they seed it again every couple of years. A nice thing about the reservoir is you can walk all the way around it since there aren't any streams coming in or out.

Sawyer got to the reservoir half an hour before Bill and I did. He had already caught a bluegill and a five-

pound rainbow trout. We found a different spot.

After an hour and a half, I still had nothing. I don't think Bill's wading in the water helped. ("Don't worry; I'll wade stealth," he'd said.)

It was then that Bill let out an exclamation. (I think it was "Zooks!") I asked him what was up.

"I think I saw Chris Franklin by Dwayne's fishing spot across the lake," Bill said.

"It can't be Chris," I said. "He's banned from this competition."

Last year Chris had tried to fish using cherry bombs. The judges told him he couldn't compete for the next three years.

I couldn't see Chris, so I didn't think about it until later.

The contest ended at 11:00 AM and we went to Sawyer's site. He had done pretty well; he had caught another trout and a good- sized walleye.

"That's pretty good, Sawyer," I said.

"Do you think it's good enough to win?" Sawyer asked.

"Not this year!" It was Dwayne, carrying a line with some very large fish. "I have proved the power of magnetism in fishing!"

"That is quite a catch there," said Bill. "Let's see, you have three rainbow trout, and that is a sizable walleye. And a Chinook salmon, and if I'm not mistaken, that's a blackfin tuna!"

"I think I caught some of the biggest fish ever caught here," Dwayne said. "Of course, next year, when everyone has one of these fish magnets, they'll all be catching fish like this. You can buy one now, Sawyer, for $19.95. Next Monday I'll probably be charging $20."

"So how long did it take you to catch those fish?" Bill asked.

"Oh, about ten minutes," Dwayne said. "The rest of the time I was playing video games on my portable."

(He did have a sweet Pocket Blaster 2500 with the newest *Space Stuff* game, *Slugtop's Revenge*. I could have played video games this whole time and caught just as many fish.)

"I think you cheated," Sawyer said.

"What did you say?" Dwayne asked.

"You heard me. I think you cheated. I don't know how to prove it, but somehow I will."

"Why don't you prove it with your fists?" Dwayne taunted. Dwayne was about a foot taller than Sawyer.

"Sawyer, sit down," Bill thundered. "I think we should just let Dwayne go to the judges. Let the best man win."

Sawyer and Dwayne were suddenly still. One didn't often hear a testy warthog. Then Dwayne smiled.

"Yeah," Dwayne said. "Listen to the pig." And he walked off with his fish.

"He's cheating somehow," Sawyer said. "We've got to do something."

"You have great patience when you're fishing," Bill said. "You need the Holy Spirit's fruit of patience in the rest of your life. If you wait, you will find the judges aren't too impressed with Dwayne's catch."

Bill was right. The judges disqualified Dwayne, and Sawyer won the contest. Sawyer shared some fried trout with me that night, and Bill had all the leftover bait.

How did Bill know that Dwayne would be disqualified? And what is the fruit of patience?

☞ **Turn to page 96 to find out!**

Chapter 6

The Attack of the Mutant Fruit

"Utterly silly!" Bill said, throwing down the comic in disgust.

Usually Bill and I look at the new *Phil the Warthog* comics together, but I was busy with homework, so Bill was reading it first.

My parents said I could do my homework over at Bill's office. Usually I can study pretty well there, but it was tougher this time because Bill kept muttering, "Preposterous," "Impossible," or "Utterly outlandish!"

"Aren't Mike's comics usually a bit silly?" I asked.

"Well, of course," Bill said, "but super soldiers, time machines and historical inaccuracies are one thing. An attack by deadly produce is just too absurd."

Well, that caught my attention. I put my math book aside (I'm afraid it doesn't take much to get me to put down my math textbook) to read the comic.

The opening panels pictured Phil the Warthog and his superior, Shady Thompkins, in their top-secret headquarters. Both characters looked nervous.

PHIL: How much more do you think the building can take?

SHADY: Not much. What is that fiend, Dr. Werner von Doomcough* up to now?

("*Doomcough is the evil scientist whose genetic experiments turned Phil from an ordinary warthog into the talking super soldier rescued by Shady Thompkins. See Issue #1," the editor's note read.)

The next panels showed strawberries and watermelons bombarding the building.

PHIL: How can ordinary fruit do such damage?

SHADY: That's not ordinary fruit, Phil. The evil Dr. Doomcough has gone from genetically altering animals to engineering fruit.

PHIL: What has he done to the fruit?

SHADY: Watch that monitor, Phil! Those are no ordinary strawberries, they're exploding strawberries! Those watermelons must weigh over 250 pounds.

PHIL: Attacking fruit. I've never heard of such a thing!

SHADY: Well, there was that tomato attack in the 1970s, but it was nothing like this!

The building couldn't take the pounding any longer. Cracks in the roof began to appear. And grapefruit came through those cracks. The grapefruit began squirting.

SHADY: Run, Phil, run! Those grapefruit aren't just squirting juice, they're squirting sulfuric acid.

PHIL: I thought you'd trained me to face any foe, Shady, but I guess you didn't train me to face deadly fruit.

The next picture showed the mobile headquarters of Dr. Werner von Doomcough. It was a bus rigged up as a hothouse, with a giant catapult on the roof.

Inside, the evil Doctor and his weasely assistant, Mortimer the Weasel, were talking.

MORTIMER: Doctor, surely the acid-squirting grapefruit have taken out Shady and his warthog ally.

DOCTOR: Don't be so sure, my devious friend. I think, to be sure, we'll send our newest creation.

MORTIMER: Not, not…the brainiac bananas!

DOCTOR: Yes, the brainiac bananas! Not only can they walk, run and throw themselves through the air, they can even think.

MORTIMER: No!

DOCTOR: Yes! Anywhere Shady and Phil try to run, they will find banana peels beneath their feet. Bwaha-ha-ha-ha!

MORTIMER: Why are we attacking them again?

DOCTOR: Because it's mean. And mean is our business.

The next picture showed the mighty catapult launching bunch after bunch of bananas through the air. The bananas landed inside the secret headquarters.

SHADY: Oh no, Phil! I believe we are facing even more deadly foes. Those are brainiac bananas!

Then a caption box read, "Will Shady and Phil survive the fighting fruit? Don't miss the next exciting adventure!"

"Well, what do you think?" Bill said.

"It is pretty silly," I told Bill.

"I think it's one of the dumbest things I've ever read. And I'm going to tell Mike that when he comes over."

"Isn't that a little harsh?" I asked.

"It's truthful," Bill said.

It wasn't long until Mike did come over. Bill was in the back, so I answered the door. Mike and I talked about homework until Bill came out.

"So, Bill, did you read the new issue of *Phil the Warthog*? I tried to do some new things, take some chances. So, what did you think?"

Mike looked excited. You could tell he was very pleased with his new creation.

I looked at Bill. I could tell that he was about to launch into the same kind of vicious attack on the comic he had made before.

I decided to act. I gave Bill a quick sidekick to the shin that I hoped Mike wouldn't notice.

Warthogs don't like kicks to the shins. I doubt many creatures do, but it got Bill to look at me. I looked back, hoping he would understand what I was trying to get through to him.

"Ouch!" Bill said.

"Sorry," I said.

"Why did you do that?" Bill asked.

Then he said, "Oh," and his voice changed. "About your comic, Mike. It wasn't quite my cup of tea, but it, um, was lively. I could tell you'd worked hard on it."

"Thanks, Bill," Mike said. "Is there anything you

would have done differently with it?"

"Well, I prefer a bit more realism," said Bill, "though of course, one of the so-called mutant fruit in the comic was quite credible."

"Yeah, maybe I did get a little out there," Mike said. "Thanks for reading it, Bill."

"I liked it," I said.

"Thanks, Nick. See you later," and Mike took off.

"I owe you thanks, too, Nick. I'm afraid I was tempted to be rather mean to Mike."

"Yeah, but I think you went overboard the other way. Why did you say one of those fruits was possible? That's crazy talk."

"Not only possible, but real. Thanks, Nick, for reminding me of a more important fruit, the fruit of kindness."

Which of the fruits in the comic is real? And what is the fruit of kindness?

 Turn to page 98 to find out!

Chapter 7

The Case of Good Deeds, Inc.

Kenny Turner knocked on my door and said two words when I opened it, "No mud."

When I asked, "Whatever are you talking about?" he told me.

"I'm telling you there was no mud on the car when I finished washing it this morning. My dad told me I had to wash our car before I went to play in the park. So I did.

"When I came home from the park, there was Chris Franklin, finishing up washing our car."

"The car you had already washed?" I asked.

"Yep. My dad came out of the house and asked me why I hadn't washed the car. I said I did, but he said I must not have done too good a job."

"What did he mean by that?"

Kenny shook his head, "My dad said Chris knocked on the door and asked if there were any towels he could use to dry the car. Chris said he noticed the car was dirty, so he thought he'd do the neighborly thing and wash it."

"But you had washed it, right?" I asked.

"Chris said he was walking by our house and noticed our car was all muddy. He showed Dad dirty rags he said he had used to scrub the car. So my Dad said I wasn't getting my allowance for the week since I hadn't done my job. He gave Chris $5!"

"But there was no mud on the car when you left it?"

"No mud at all."

It sounded like this situation needed some investigation, so Kenny and I went to get Bill. Then we went to see Chris Franklin.

Chris welcomed us in. "Glad to see you all," Chris said. "Here, each of you, take a card."

We each took a card reading, "Good Deeds, Inc., Chris X. Franklin, President."

"So what is 'Good Deeds, Inc.'?" Bill asked after

Chris showed us to seats on the Franklins' living room couch.

"Oh, Good Deeds, Incorporated? It's my new business, if you care to call it that. I just go about town looking for good deeds to do, and I do them."

"Yeah, right," smirked Kenny. "Good deeds, sure."

"Of course," Chris assured us. "And speaking of good deeds, can I get any of you something to drink, ice water or fruit juice, perhaps?"

"We just need answers to a few questions. What was the condition of the Turners' car when you saw it this morning?"

"Why, it was just covered with mud and filth," Chris said. "As President of Good Deeds, Inc., I felt I must do something about it, so I cleaned it up."

"But I had washed the car before you came by," Kenny protested.

"Perhaps someone got it dirty after that," Chris suggested. "There are some troublemakers in the neighborhood. Or perhaps you didn't do as good a job as you thought."

At that, Kenny looked like he was about to

explode, so Bill quickly asked Chris another question.

"Are there any other people you have assisted?" Bill asked.

"Oh, yes," said Chris. "If you keep your eyes open, you'll see all kinds of people who need help. For instance, just yesterday, Friday, I was walking to school, and I noticed someone had knocked over the Sbranas' trash cans."

"The Sbranas, that elderly couple on my street?" I asked.

"Why, yes. Do you know them? Anyway, it was just 8:00 AM, and school doesn't start till 8:30, so I figured I had time to clean it up."

"You cleaned it up all on your own?" Bill asked.

"Yes, I did," said Chris. "I was able to clean up most of the things easily, the newspapers, plastic bottles and such. There were coffee grounds spilled on the sidewalk, though. I knocked on the Sbranas' door and asked if I could borrow a broom and dustpan to sweep up the coffee grounds."

"And did they pay you for your trouble?" Bill asked.

"As a matter of fact, they may have given me a few dollars. We at Good Deeds, Inc., have discovered that when you do something for others, they often do something for you in return."

As we left, Kenny asked Bill if he had learned anything useful.

"Not yet," Bill said. "But I think we may learn something from visiting the Sbranas."

We knocked on the Sbranas' door. I could see someone looking through the peephole for what seemed a very long time before Mrs. Sbrana opened the door.

"Oh, you're that Sayga boy from down the street. Nick, isn't it? Could you introduce me to your friends?"

I introduced Bill and Kenny. Mrs. Sbrana couldn't take her eyes off Bill. As Mr. Sbrana entered the room, she whispered in my ear, "Does your poor friend have some kind of skin disease?"

Before I could answer, Bill began investigating.

"Mr. Sbrana, I understand Chris Franklin cleaned up your garbage yesterday?"

"Yes, quite helpful. I don't know who knocked over those cans: dogs or perhaps some of these darn neighborhood kids. No offense, Nick, we didn't suspect you.

"Good that boy came along. Might not have noticed the spilled trash before the trash truck came at 9:00."

"I thought the trash truck came at 6:00. Don't they always wake us with that awful racket?" Mrs. Sbrana asked.

"No, the 6:00 AM pickup is for our recycling," Mr. Sbrana said. "They pick up our garbage at 9:00 AM, so it's good that boy came along."

As we left, Kenny said, "Well, that sure didn't do us any good."

"On the contrary," said Bill, "we got the proof we need that Chris didn't do such a good deed at the Sbranas'. Therefore, he probably didn't do a good deed at your house either."

"What proof?" Kenny asked.

"We'll give the evidence to Chris, and I'm sure he'll agree to apologize to all the people he supposedly helped with Good Deeds, Inc. Perhaps he can start learning what it really means to do good."

What proof did Bill have? And what does it really mean to do good?

☞ Turn to page 100 to find out!

Chapter 8

The Case of the Stolen Still Life

"You have to admit, the painting came out pretty well," I said to Bill. "You would never guess you were wearing a bathing suit."

"He did capture a bit of the warthog majesty," Bill admitted.

It had taken a lot of convincing to get Bill to pose for the painting. Mike Reed needed a painting of an animal as one in a series of paintings for an Art Institute contest.

Bill had wanted to pose in his new gray flannel suit. Mike said the judges would expect the animals in the pictures to be, um, more naturally dressed. Bill wore a bathing suit and posed behind a bush, so he looked like a warthog in the wild.

The contest's first place prize is a $2,500 scholarship to the Art Institute. Entrants have to paint a portrait of a person, an abstract (interesting design picture), a landscape (or scenery picture), an animal portrait and a still life (whatever that is).

Mike had dropped the picture at Bill's office earlier in the day, after the judging, so I was surprised when he knocked on Bill's door again.

"Hey, Mike, great job on the picture of Bill! I really like that landscape painting of the reservoir, too."

"I've been impressed," said Bill. "But what brings you here again already?"

"Nothing good, I'm afraid. I think someone stole my still life," Mike said.

(This sounded like bad news, but at least I'd find out what a still life was.)

"Tell us the story," Bill said.

Mike started with what we knew: he had already entered four paintings in the contest. The portrait of his father was ranked second, but his landscape, abstract and his painting of Bill in the animal contest had all ranked first. If he did even a decent still life, he was bound to win the contest.

So I had my chance to ask, "What is a still life?"

"It's a painting of inanimate objects. I guess I could have painted action figures, but traditionally, people paint a vase of flowers or a bowl of fruit. I went with the fruit."

"What happened to your painting?" Bill asked.

"I was working on it in the garage today, and was about finished. I always put about an hour a day into painting or drawing.

"Anyway, the phone rang, and I went inside to answer it. Whoever called hung up when I answered. When I went back to the garage, the painting was gone."

"When is the deadline for the painting?" I asked.

"Tomorrow. No way I can get anything decent done by then. I've been working on this one for a week."

"Do you have any idea who might have taken it?" Bill asked.

"Well," Mike paused and thought, "there are a lot of kids in the contest, but the kid with the best shot of winning is Josh Malone."

"Chris Franklin's friend? Figures," I said.

"He did get second place all the times I got first.

Though there are rumors he had help," Mike said.

We were off to Josh's place.

Josh came to the door. "Hey, Mikey, Tan Toad, Babe."

"That's Mike, Ten Toes and Mr. Warthog to you," I said.

"Whatever," Josh said. "Why you here?"

"I'd like to see your still life," Mike said.

"Not quite done. I work by inspiration, got an idea this morning and am almost done," Josh said. "I guess you can see it before it gets the blue ribbon tomorrow."

Josh led us to his bedroom, which was surprisingly tidy. His bed was made and on the floor there were just a couple of socks. In the corner was an easel with a painting of fruit. A bowl of fruit, which matched the painting perfectly, sat on a small table.

"So, how long have you been working on this painting?" Bill asked.

"All day," Josh said. "I set up the fruit how I wanted it and then went to work. It's quick drying paint, but I need to add a few last touches."

I looked at the painting and then at the fruit on the table. There was a pineapple near the back, a couple of bananas, a pear and an apple with a slice out of it.

The painting captured the shapes and colors of the objects perfectly: the yellow and brown of the pineapple, the yellow of the banana, the green of the pear, the red of the apple skin and the white of the apple flesh.

"That's my painting," Mike said.

"I don't think so," Josh replied. "I used my digital camera moments ago to take a picture of the easel, paints and fruit bowl. I'll put the pictures on my blog online, and everyone will know it's my work."

"Your digital camera," Mike said. "There are rumors you took digital pictures, printed them and painted over them for your previous pictures."

"People will say all kinds of things," Josh said. "But you have to admit I certainly captured this bowl of fruit with my paints."

"I do admit that the painting and the bowl of fruit look remarkably similar," Bill said.

"Thank you," Josh said. "At least someone recognizes art."

"I was saying I recognized fraud," Bill said. "You stole Mike's painting. He has been as faithful to his art as you have been unfaithful to the truth."

"What are you talking about?" Josh said.

Bill took Josh to another room, and when they came back, Josh gave the painting back to Mike.

As we left, Bill said, "Josh, you should worry less about bowls of fruit, and more about the fruit of faithfulness."

How could Bill prove Josh was lying? What is the fruit of faithfulness?

☞ Turn to page 102 to find out!

The Case of the Nose Job

"Take the Guess Work out of Nose Picking," read the sign by Seth Austin's project at the science fair. His project was pretty cool, much cooler than my soil sample comparisons. (Bill thought I should do a project on warthogs, but I told him rules forbid the use of animals.)

Seth had come up with an invention that is basically a miniature camera mounted on a handle. It allows someone to look at what he or she is doing while nostril clearing. I know it's gross, but it's handy.

If the science fair jury had any misgivings about the yuck factor of Seth's project, they must have put them aside, because the Visually Aided Nasal

Obstruction Device took first place in the fair.

When I told Bill about Seth's project, he said it was interesting, but "Of course, we warthogs do nothing as disgusting as nose picking."

I asked if it was really an issue of warthog manners, or more the fact their hooves don't fit in their nostrils.

"Perhaps, Nick, both of those things are factors. It does sound like it would be an interesting device to examine."

That opportunity came up sooner than we expected. Seth called me on the phone.

"Hey Nick, I just got a kinda weird call. This person said he was from the AMA. He told me that the AMA had heard about my invention and needed to examine the NoseCam to see if it met safety regulations."

"What's the AMA?" I asked.

"The American Medical Association. The person on the phone said the AMA was going to send a doctor to my house to check out the NoseCam."

"So you think something is funny about this?"

"Maybe. My parents won't be home, and I don't want to let a stranger come to the house when I'm alone. This doctor is coming to my house tomorrow at

4:00 PM. Do you think you could be here with your police dog friend?"

"You mean my warthog detective friend?"

"Yeah, whatever. Maybe you should come a little early."

We were at Seth's at 3:30. The micro camera fascinated Bill. "Why it's the size of a piece of rice! I could do amazing surveillance work with this!"

"Bill, we'll talk about your sleuthing supplies later. Let's figure out what to do with this case."

We decided that Seth would meet with this guy in the living room, and Bill and I could listen unobserved in the dining room next to it. There was a knock on the door at exactly 4:00 PM.

"Good afternoon, I'm Dr. Anton Proboscis. I am here today as a representative of the American Medical Association and the Food and Drug Administration. Now let's have a look at that invention of yours."

Seth brought out the NoseCam and showed Dr. Proboscis how it was used. He explained how it was to be used with caution and showed the booklet of safety tips.

"Well, Seth, this is an interesting little tool you've made here. You might really have a future in the medical field.

"I'm afraid I'll need to take this invention with me so it can be examined for safety in our labs."

"I can't let you have it now," Seth said. "This is the prototype, the only one I have. If you give me a few weeks I can make another and you can examine it."

"I don't have the leeway to give you those few weeks, Seth. I need to take the NoseCam today for inspection. You allowed this camera to be used on fellow classmates, which amounts to practicing medicine without a license."

"Kids pick their noses all the time! That is not practicing medicine."

"Seth, I am a specialist in nasal medicine. I am also a representative of the United States government, and it is imperative that you hand this device over to me."

"Like I said, I can't turn this over till you give me time to make another prototype. I also have to send my blueprints to the patent office."

"Do you have wax in your ears, boy? I'm a nose specialist, so I don't clean wax from ears, but you will turn the device and your plans over to me, today."

Bill didn't wait any longer. He grabbed my arm and we went in the living room.

"What is this creature here?" Dr. Proboscis exclaimed. "I'm a doctor, not a veterinarian."

"And I'm a detective, not a creature," Bill said. "I don't believe you are even a doctor. I believe you are a fraud."

"Seth, I assume you will not listen to this, this, thing. I am a doctor and I need to take your device for important medical reasons."

"I think," said Bill, "You want to take the device not for the AMA or the FDA, but for M-O-N-E-Y. I think you want to steal Seth's invention and claim it as your own, and that is why you came. And by the way, my name is Bill."

"All right, Bill. Maybe there are some monetary factors involved. But you have to understand that medicine is a rough business and you have to take the advantage where you can."

"Then perhaps you need to bring the Holy Spirit's fruit of gentleness to counter that rough business. But as I said before, your words have shown you are not who you say you are. I suggest you leave this property before I call the police and you find yourself under

arrest for impersonating a doctor and a government official."

"Dr." Proboscis left quite quickly. And Seth went to work on patenting the NoseCam.

What did Proboscis say that showed he was not who he said he was? And what is this fruit of gentleness that Bill was talking about?

☞ Turn to page 104 to find out!

Chapter 10

The Case of the Football Fanatic

You could say Jayden Patrick is a football fan, in the same way you could say cotton candy has sugar in it or the sky is blue on a clear day. All Jayden thought and talked about was football, especially about his favorite college team, the North State Badgers.

He knew all the records and statistics from the 57 years the Badgers had played, he knew on what pro teams former Badgers played, and he knew the favorite pizza toppings of the Badgers' coach, Lou "Buck" Sternwell.

This goes a little way toward explaining why Jayden was so upset when Chris Franklin began to spread rumors that the Badgers' games were fixed.

"I'm going to tackle Chris so hard that his head will go to Friday and his feet will still be back on Monday," Jayden told me.

"Calm down, guy," I said to him. "It wouldn't be the right thing to do. It especially would not be the right thing to do now, on the playground during recess. You don't need that kind of teacher trouble."

"But, Nick, I'm so mad!" Jayden shouted.

"I know, I know. Calm down and tell me what happened."

"OK. But after I tell you, I'm going after Chris. You see, I got to school early and I was tossing the pigskin—"

"Pigskin?" I asked.

"You know, a pigskin is a football. Anyway, I was tossing it with some of my friends, and we were talking about this weekend's Badgers game."

"Didn't the Badgers slaughter the Otters this weekend?"

"Oh yeah, Nick, they held the Otters scoreless in the first half and ended up beating them 42-3. So anyway, Chris Franklin came up, saying he had bet money on the game and won big bucks."

"It's not legal to gamble on games, is it?"

"No, of course not. But he bet other kids at school, and he said he had known the Badgers would win because he had inside information about the game."

"What inside information?"

"Chris said that all the college games are rigged, and there's a website that gives all the scores in advance."

"No way."

"Yeah, well, there were a couple of guys from Chris's gang there backing him up. They said that they used Chris's information and bet other kids on the game. Chris said he knew the scores for the five remaining games of the season, and if we paid him, we could see the scores on this sheet of paper he had."

"Doesn't sound too likely. It would mean that all the coaches and players would have to be in on it."

"Exactly," said Jayden. "He said it's just like the wrestling on TV. That would mean even Coach Sternwell is in on it."

"Wait," I said. "The wrestling on TV is fixed?"

"Could you talk to your detective friend about this?" Jayden asked. "I need to know whether or not this is true. I need to know whether I need to rip the Badger posters off my wall or something off Chris's face."

I assured Jayden that we could talk to Bill before any ripping began.

Bill listened to Jayden's story. (Again, Jayden said he was tossing the "pigskin" and I told Bill it wasn't what he thought, and he said he knew what it meant, but would really prefer Jayden used another phrase. Jayden said he would because if someone talked about passing the "human skin" it would gross him out.)

The three of us went to see Chris.

"You are all so naïve," Chris said. "Does it surprise you that when big money is involved, like in college football, they have to plan these things out? Of course the games are rigged."

"Coach Sternwell wouldn't go along with it," Jayden muttered.

"He's just a crook like the rest of them," Chris said.

Bill had to throw himself in front of Jayden so Jayden wouldn't throw himself on Chris.

"Calm down," said Bill. "All right, Chris, you say you have the scores for the remaining games of the season. If that is so, perhaps we can see them."

"Of course you can," said Chris. "Just pay me the

two dollars per game that every other kid has paid."

"Kids have paid two dollars a game?" I asked, shocked at the stupidity of some of my fellow Elm Street students. "Do you guarantee these scores?"

"I just can't do that," Chris said. "The problem is, word might get out about the website giving the information, and the teams might have to change their game plans so people won't catch on that the games are rigged."

"Can I see the website?" Bill asked.

"So you could cut in on my business?" Chris said. "I don't think so."

"I will pay you ten dollars for all five scores," Bill said.

"OK, but as I said," said Chris, "I can't give you the money back if the scores don't come out exactly right."

"You aren't really going to give this maggot money, are you, Mr. Warthog?" Jayden asked.

Out of Bill's wallet came the ten dollars, and Chris handed him a sheet with these scores:

North State Badgers 35, Clear Lake Vipers 14
North State Badgers 9, Walleye University 24
North State Badgers 12, Howell University Owls 1
North State Badgers 27, Superior River Raccoons 7
North State Badgers 24, West State Mambas 16

When Jayden saw the list, he said, "We're going to beat the Black Mambas? Cool."

Bill turned to Chris and said, "Please give me my money back. This list is a fraud. And you'll need to give money back to any student you took it from."

"It's a fraud?" Jayden exclaimed. "Let me at him."

"NO!" said Bill. "Let me talk to him alone."

Bill did and got his money back. And Chris agreed to go with Jayden to return the money to all the other students.

Before they left, Jayden asked, "How did you know that list was a fraud?"

"I'll tell you," said Bill. "But there is something you need to learn about even more: the fruit of self-control."

How did Bill know the list was a fraud? And what is this fruit of self-control?

☞Turn to page 106 to find out!

The Case of the Maltese Fruit

Q: *How did Bill know Chris was growing lies and not gumballs?*

A: Chris claimed to be a plant expert, but what he said proved otherwise. When listing the vegetables he grew, he included tomatoes, avocados and kiwis. Tomatoes are fruit, even though they are cooked with vegetables. Avocados and kiwis, while green inside, are also fruit.

Chris eventually confessed he was not an expert in horticulture and that his gumball plant was a fake.

Q: *What is this fruit of the Spirit Bill was talking about?*

A: In the Bible there is a book called Galatians. It is a letter that a man named Paul wrote to a church. (Paul was an apostle, which means he traveled around telling people about Jesus Christ and starting churches, so he is sometimes called the Apostle Paul.) In the fifth chapter of Galatians, Paul writes about the fruit of the Spirit.

Paul talks about rotten things we should avoid (jealousy, fits of rage, selfishness, etc.), and then contrasts them with good qualities he calls fruit.

Paul probably got the idea from Jesus. In Luke 6:43, Jesus said, "No good tree bears bad fruit, nor does a bad tree bear good fruit" and in Luke 6:45, "The good man brings good things out of the good stored up in his heart."

The fruit of the Spirit describes the qualities people show if they let God's Spirit rule in their lives. But what are those qualities? Bill will let us know the details in the stories to come.

The Case of the Counterfeit Valentines

Q: *How did Bill know Ryan was the Valentine blackmailer?*

A: Bill's proof that Ryan was lying was the story about the official United States postage stamp honoring Digger Graves and the other wrestlers.

The U.S. Postal Service's policy is that any person commemorated on a stamp must have been dead for ten years or more. U.S. presidents are the only exceptions. Living wrestlers do not qualify as stamp contenders.

Q: *And what is the fruit of the Spirit kind of love?*

A: Paul ranked love first in his list of the fruit of the Spirit in Galatians 5:22-23. Paul gave a very full description of the kind of love he was thinking of in 1 Corinthians 13.

That love is an unselfish love, considering others before yourself. Jacob didn't "like" Ashley, but she was a friend. So his first concern was for Ashley's feelings.

When a lot of people think of love, they think of romantic love ("sitting in the tree, K-I-S-S-I-N-G," and so on). But the everyday thinking of others before yourself kind of love is what Paul was thinking about, and Bill was too.

The Case of the Stolen Jokes

Q: *What did Steven write that showed he was the true author of the comedy act?*

A: Steven knew the original "What's black and white and red all over?" joke.

Perhaps it should be spelled "read all over" since the original answer to the joke is "a newspaper."

Q: *Why did Bill want to save Steven's joy as well as Steven's comedy act?*

A: Jokes provide laughs and fun. Joy, the fruit of joy, is something different. Or maybe Bill would say joy is

something more.

Laughs and fun come and go. It's hard (and perhaps not wise) to laugh during a tough math test. And it's not easy to have fun with, say, stomach flu.

But if we trust in God, and have His Spirit, then we have the fruit of joy in our lives. It's a happiness that doesn't come and go. And that's no joke.

Phil the Warthog Goes West

Q: *How did Phil know Bart Blackhate owned the cattle that ruined Farmer McCoy's fruit trees?*

A: Phil (and Bill) knew the cattle belonged to the Blackhates because of the description of the brand.

Bart Blackhate said their brand was the "Bar Twenty." Farmer McCoy described the brand as two "Xs" with a line underneath.

The Roman numeral "X" stands for ten. And the line under the "XX" is called a bar. So Farmer McCoy had been describing the Blackhate brand.

But Phil (and Bill) were more concerned about looking for peace.

Q: *Why look for the fruit of peace?*

A: Peace is another part of the fruit of the Spirit that Paul wrote about in Galatians 5:22-23.

Paul also wrote about peace in Romans 12:18 in his letter to the Christians in Rome. To paraphrase

Paul, we should live at peace with everyone as much as we can.

You'll probably find in life that things work out better if you aren't always looking to get your own way. Concern yourself with what other people need, too.

Peace is not only important in the Old West, but at your school, in your house, everywhere you go.

So for now, Peace Out!

The Case of the Magnetic Bait

Q: *Why was Bill sure Dwayne's catch of fish would not impress the judges as much as Sawyer's?*

A: Bill was confident the judges would disqualify Dwayne because of the fish he claimed to have caught. Walleye, trout and bluegill are all fresh water fish that are likely to be seeded in a reservoir.

But salmon is a migratory fish, very unlikely to be found in such a place where no streams lead in or out. And the tuna is a saltwater fish; blackfin tuna is caught in the ocean.

Bill had seen Chris Franklin. Chris bought the fish and brought them to Dwayne. They bought magnets for two dollars and planned to sell them as fish-contest-winning bait for twenty dollars.

Instead, Dwayne and Chris were stuck with several boxes full of magnets.

Q: *Why was Bill so hooked on the fruit of patience?*

A: The fruit of patience is another part of the fruit of the Spirit.

There are times when life is hard and circumstances are difficult. But God can give us the patience to wait through tough times.

It's also important to learn to be patient with other people, because there are probably others who are being patient with you.

The Attack of the Mutant Fruit

Q: *Which of the mutant fruit was believable?*

A: Watermelons can grow to amazing sizes. A 136-pound watermelon, grown in Hope, Arkansas, was given as a gift to President Calvin Coolidge.

That's puny compared to watermelons grown along the Tigris River, which have been known to reach as much as 275 pounds.

Q: *What about the fruit of kindness?*

A: Bill was right that one of the truly important fruits is that of kindness.

Bill was tempted to be as mean as Dr. Werner von Doomcough to Mike about the comic. But Nick helped Bill remember the need for kindness.

There are times we may have to

disagree with others, or correct someone's mistake or even criticize someone else's work.

But even in those situations, we need to find a way to be kind.

Kindness is part of the fruit of the Spirit, and it's never out of season.

The Case of Good Deeds, Inc.

Q: *What evidence did Bill have that Chris's deeds were bad?*

A: Chris said he had cleaned up the Sbranas' garbage around 8:00 AM before the 9:00 AM garbage pick up. He said he cleaned up newspapers and plastic bottles.

Newspapers and plastic bottles would surely have been in the recycling, which Mr. Sbrana said was picked up earlier, at 6:00 AM.

Chris had spilled coffee grounds so it would appear he had cleaned up a big mess. At Kenny's house, he got the car wet and showed Kenny's father muddy towels.

Q: *What does it mean to really have the fruit of goodness?*

A: The deeds that come from the goodness Paul

wrote about in Galatians 5:22 aren't there for show just so others will do good things for you. With God's Spirit

working in our lives, we'll do good without regard for consequences.

And doing good for God will put you in good company.

The Case of the Stolen Still Life

Q: *How could Bill prove Josh was lying?*

A: Bill knew Josh was lying because the painting matched the fruit too well, especially the colors. The flesh of apple in the painting was just as white as the apple on the table.

That was the problem. If Josh had been working on the painting for hours, as he said, the apple flesh would have turned brown already.

Josh had taken the painting from Mike's garage, then set up the fruit just before Bill, Nick and Mike got there so he could claim the painting was his.

Q: *What did faithfulness have to do with this case?*

A: Mike was very faithful with his art, taking time for it every day. Josh was not faithful with his art. He especially wasn't faithful with the truth.

Paul included faithfulness in his list of the fruit of the Spirit, because faithfulness to God and others is very important.

By the way, Mike won the contest. And he let Bill keep his portrait, after a few modifications. Mike added a trench coat and fedora.

The Case of the Nose Job

Q: *What did Dr. Proboscis say that proved to Bill he wasn't telling the truth?*

A: Dr. Proboscis said he was a nose specialist and didn't deal with ears. There is no such thing. If you look in the yellow pages of the telephone book under medical specialties, you'll find listings for "ear, nose and throat" specialists.

Since those parts of the body are so closely connected, no doctor would know about only one of the three.

Bill called the American Medical Association and confirmed that Dr. Proboscis was a fraud who wanted to get his hands on Seth's invention.

Q: *What is the fruit of gentleness?*

A: The fruit of gentleness is another aspect of the

fruit of the Spirit Paul wrote about in Galatians 5.

Just as it was important that Seth's invention was gentle with a sensitive part of the body, we need to be

gentle with other people. Especially with those who are younger or more sensitive.

The fruit of gentleness is an important fruit to pick (as opposed to picking noses, which I suppose we have talked about long enough).

The Case of the Football Fanatic

Q: *Why was Bill sure Chris's list was fake?*

A: Bill could tell Chris's list was fake because of one of the scores. The score was Badgers 12, Owls 1. Some scores are less likely than others, but a team cannot score only one point in football.

Q: *What is the fruit of self-control?*

A: Self-control is the last on Paul's list of the fruit of the Spirit. It is important that we think before we react

 to hard situations. We can't let our emotions make our decisions.

We should direct our decisions instead by sound thinking and God's Spirit, though emotion may play a part.

We've all heard about the importance of good nutrition. And it is certainly important not to eat too much sugar and junk food and to get enough protein, vitamins, minerals, vegetables, fruit, etc.

But more than any part of our diet plan, it is important to have the fruit of the Spirit in our lives.

"Crime is like a cockroach, but not as tasty."

– Bill the Warthog

Get more Bill with *Full Metal Trench Coat*, the first book in the **Bill the Warthog Mysteries** series. Can you solve the crimes for Nick and his friends before Bill does?

ISBN 10: 1-58411-068-6
ISBN 13: 978-1-58411-068-2

"Cracking cases? Easy. Flossing is another story."
– Bill the Warthog

Test your detective skills alongside Bill and Nick. In their second book, *Guarding the Tablets of Stone,* the friends put ten exciting cases under the magnifying glass.

ISBN 10: 1-58411-073-2
ISBN 13: 978-1-58411-073-6